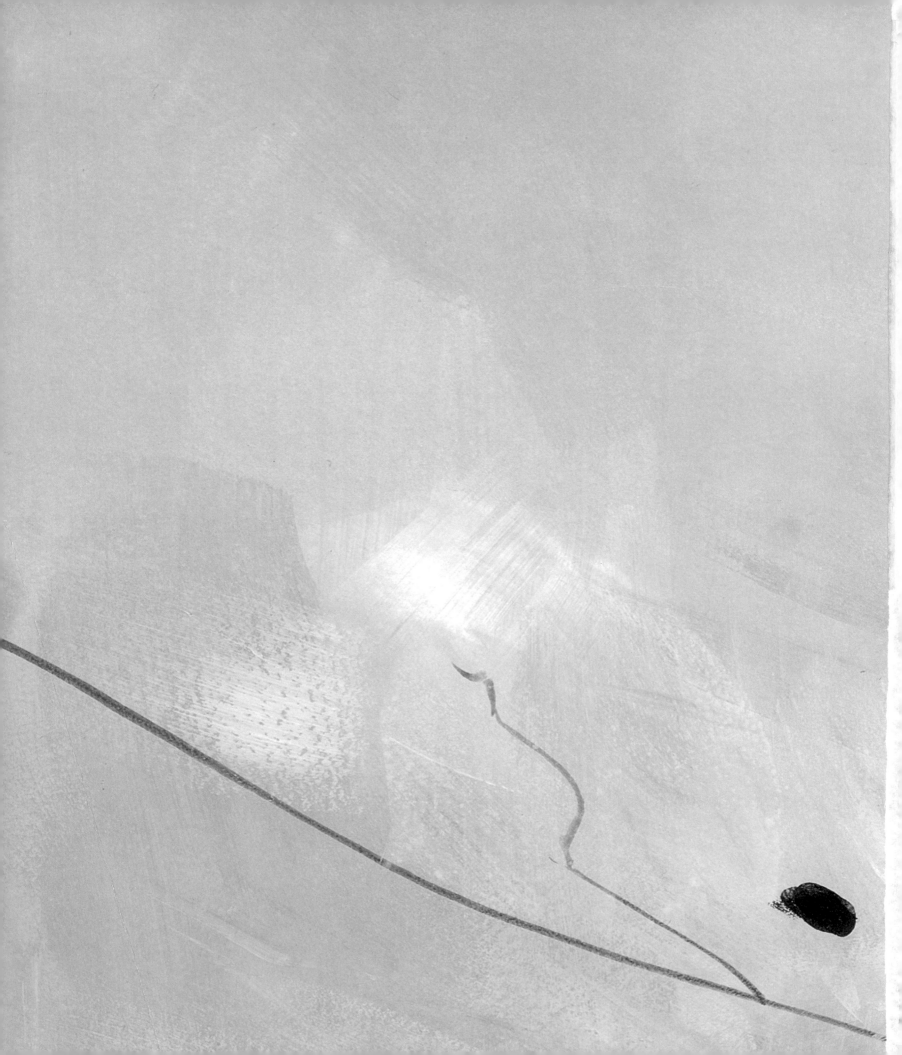

To Ellen, who helped me sing,
and Michelle, who taught me to fly.
—J. B.

This is for all of the positive people
who have been the "seed magic"
in my life. Thank you.
—C. R. W.

Ω

Published by
PEACHTREE PUBLISHERS
1700 Chattahoochee Avenue
Atlanta, Georgia 30318-2112
www.peachtree-online.com

Text ©2011 by Jane Buchanan
Illustrations ©2011 by Charlotte Riley-Webb

Art direction by Loraine M. Joyner
Illustrations created in acrylic on 100% rag archival paper.
Title and bylines typeset in International Typeface Corporation's Pablo
by Trevor Pettit; text typeset in Beach-Normal.

Printed in October 2011 by Tien Wah Press in Singapore
10 9 8 7 6 5 4 3 2 1
First Edition

Library of Congress Cataloging-in-Publication Data

Buchanan, Jane, 1956-
  Seed magic / written by Jane Buchanan ; illustrated by Charlotte Riley-Webb.
     p. cm.
  Summary: Rose takes a gift from the crazy old Birdman and discovers that
even in the bleak, gray city there are ways to make a beautiful
garden.
  ISBN 978-1-56145-622-2 / 1-56145-622-5
  [1. Birds—Fiction. 2. Inner cities—Fiction. 3. African Americans—a
Fiction.] I. Riley-Webb, Charlotte, ill. II. Title.
  PZ7.B877135Se 2012
  [E]—dc23
                    2011020462

Seed Magic

Jane Buchanan

illustrated by
Charlotte Riley-Webb

PEACHTREE
ATLANTA

Crazy old Birdman feeding the pigeons.

Sitting in his wheelchair,

feeding the pigeons.

Smiling and laughing. "Nnn-nn-nnn."

"What you doing, Birdman?"

Brother Toby laughing,

dancing around Birdman.

Birdman just smiles.

"Crazy old Birdman.

Birds on your shoulders,

birds on your head.

You crazy, Birdman,"

brother Natty says.

Rose says, "Why you like pigeons

so much, Birdman?"

"Why you don't?" Birdman says back.

"Look at 'em. Beautiful."

Rose looks, but she sees only pigeons.

Dirty gray pigeons,

like this dirty gray city.

"Birds not beautiful," Rose says.

"Gardens are beautiful."

She closes her eyes and sees

blue lupines,

red geraniums,

yellow sunflowers,

like in her library books.

Birdman winks,

reaches into his sack.

"Make like a bowl," he says.

And Rose does.

Birdman sprinkles a stream of seeds

black as tar,

slick as oil,

into her hands.

"Put 'em outside your window,"

Birdman says. "You grow you a garden."

"Can't grow no garden there," Rose says.

"Can with these seeds," Birdman says.

"These seeds magic?" Rose asks.

"Jack and the Beanstalk seeds?"

"Nnn-nn-nnn," Birdman laughs.

"Uh-huh. Magic all right."

All the way home, Rose doesn't drop a one.

"You crazy as Birdman," Toby says.

"Rose the Birdgirl," Natty says.

They laugh and laugh.

Rose takes those seeds and puts them on the sill.

Her brothers laugh some more, but Rose doesn't care.

"You got no dirt," Toby says.

"You got no water," Natty says.

"You can't grow nothing on a windowsill."

Rose doesn't listen. Magic seeds grow anywhere.

Rose watches. She waits. She dreams.

Blue lupines.

Red geraniums.

Yellow sunflowers.

Nothing.

Then,

one day…

Blue as lupines.

Red as geraniums.

Yellow as sunflowers.

And they are singing!

"A garden!" Rose says.

"A singing garden!"

Sitting in his wheelchair,

Birdman smiles.

"Nnn-nn-nnn," he laughs.

"Beautiful."